HAIRY HORROR

Sandra Glover

Illustrated by Kate Grove

ANDERSEN PRESS

First published in 2014 by
Andersen Press Limited
20 Vauxhall Bridge Road
London SW1V 2SA
www.andersenpress.co.uk

2 4 6 8 10 9 7 5 3 1

British Library Cataloguing in Publication Data available.

ISBN 978 1 783 44033 7

Printed and bound in Great Britain by CPI Group (UK) Ltd, Croydon CR0 4YY

For Anna-Belle, Jessica,
Dylan and Harry.

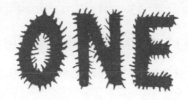

ONE

The face glowed red. Hungry eyes stared at me. Wrinkled hands grabbed my hair.

The mouth opened wider and wider.

"WaaaaaaaaAAAH!"

"Cut it out, Jamie," I said, trying to wrestle my baby brother into his sling. "We'll go and find Mum, OK?"

"Anna, watch Jamie for five minutes, will you?" Mum had said over an hour ago, when she'd wandered off clutching a can of polish and a duster.

No problem, I'm happy to spend my

Saturday mornings watching Jamie. Watching's fine when Jamie's all curled up asleep, looking cute, but once he's awake and hungry it's a nightmare.

"Mum!" I called, wandering towards the stairs.

WHAAAAHHH!!!

Surely she could hear him howling? I'd never had trouble finding Mum when we'd lived in our two-bedroom flat. Back then, of course, we didn't have a baby. It was just me and Mum. Now everything's changed. We live in a massive old house, where people can get lost for hours!

After I'd checked three of the four floors plus the huge garden, where Mum potters with her chickens and vegetables, I knew there was only one other place she could be. And I really, really didn't want to go down there.

Jamie had settled, but it wouldn't be long before he kicked off again, so I had to do it. Pushing open the door to the basement, I started picking my way down the narrow stone steps.

Going to the basement is the only part of

my new life that I don't like. I really don't mind that Mum met and married Steve. It means I have a proper dad for the first time in my life. Well, for the first time I can remember. And Steve's a vet, which is great 'cos I love animals – apart from spiders and worms.

Moving to Steve's house in the country is fine, too. The country's fun and even starting Year 5, in a school where I didn't know anyone, wasn't anything like as bad as I'd expected. I've made loads of new friends.

Some kids don't like it when a new baby comes along, but hey, I don't mind that either. What I do mind – the big, big problem in my lovely new life – lurks at the bottom of the basement stairs.

Jamie wriggled in his sling as I walked down the last few steps and stared at the door facing me. Painted dark grey, it has a large orange square in the middle with a black skull and crossbones. Lovely!

Underneath, in thick, red letters it says: KEEP OUT.

Not exactly welcoming, but that's not all – just in case someone doesn't get the message, all around the edges of the door are pictures of flames, exploding bombs, exclamation marks, lightning forks and acid dripping from a bottle onto a sizzling hand.

"That's Hal for you," I muttered to Jamie, hoping he wouldn't grow up to be as weird as his big half-brother.

Hal's teachers think he's wonderful, of course. They reckon Hal's a genius. He's got ten top-grade GCSEs and he's doing A-levels now, even though he's only just fourteen, so they could be right.

And – get this – he only has to go to school three days a week. The rest of the time he's allowed to stay at home, working on his "little projects", as he calls them, down in the basement.

"There's nothing wrong with being clever," I told Jamie. "Even mega, mega clever. It's just that Hal—"

"Goo goo eee goo," said Jamie, poking his finger towards the door.

"I suppose you're right," I said. "We ought to go in. It's not like Hal's evil or anything, is it?"

He's just "different" or "special", in Mum's words, and some of his experiments are totally weird! How someone as normal as Steve can have a son like Hal, I don't know.

Maybe Hal takes after his mum but, from what I've heard, she was fairly ordinary too. She died in a car accident five years ago, which might have turned Hal a bit strange, I suppose. Or stranger than he was already! It can't have been easy for him.

Anyway, Hal doesn't just have his laboratory in the basement – he insists on living down there as well. So behind the freaky door is his lab of horrors and, beyond that, is Hal's bedroom and shower room, which Mum's allowed into about once a month to check that it's clean.

I looked down at Jamie, who was whimpering again, gearing up for another major howl. Then, staring at those danger signs, which aren't just for show, I took a deep breath and knocked.

TWO

There was no answer. Not that I expected one. Hal never answers, even when he's in. Clutching Jamie's sling to my chest, I eased open the door, just enough to peek inside.

I've only ever seen Hal's lab a few times. It's not the sort of place you'd want to hang around in – unless you're Hal, of course. Trouble is, you never know what you're going to find or what's going to happen.

It looked peaceful enough, though. Desks full of laptops, computers, printers and phones shoved against one wall. Loads of spotlights because the narrow window doesn't let in much light – all fairly harmless.

My eyes scanned the table in the middle for signs of anything that might suddenly explode or start spewing out clouds of poisonous gas, but all I could see were four skulls, six jam jars, dozens of empty test tubes, a large bag of peanuts, a tin of pins and two bottles of liquid, which looked like cat wee –

and probably was.

The rest of the room's a miniature jungle, full of plants. Hal's into plants in a big way. Well, I told you he was weird.

I couldn't see anyone, so I pushed the door open a bit further. That's when the smell hit me.

Ugh! A mix of chemicals, damp soil, last night's chicken curry and Hal's stinky feet.

All made worse because it was so hot down there.

"Mum?" I called, looking towards the door at the back that leads to Hal's bedroom. "Hal?"

Where was everyone? Jamie was wriggling again, trying to stick his finger up my nose. No point phoning Mum's mobile, because she'd left it on the table upstairs, but I could maybe try Hal. No way was I going to risk walking through that lab to get to Hal's bedroom, especially not while I was carrying Jamie.

It looked a touch cleaner than usual but there were still millions of things to trip over. Plant pots, shoes, boxes, piles of science magazines and a big, black cat curled up underneath a huge cheese plant with leaves like shiny, green umbrellas.

Wait a minute: we don't have a black cat. We've got a three-legged ginger one, a deaf tabby and a fluffy, one-eyed white one. All unwanted moggies that Steve's brought home. So maybe this was a new one. Steve's always bringing animals home. Sometimes he finds new owners for them and sometimes they just stay.

"WaaaaaaaaaAAAH!"

I jumped as Jamie suddenly kicked off again. The cat jumped up too. Only it wasn't a cat, was it?

It was large-cat-sized.

It was furry like a cat.

But it wasn't a cat. The eyes, the legs, it was – no, it couldn't be, no way! I clutched Jamie tighter, took a step back, blinked and looked again.

My heart stopped. I swear, it totally stopped! The thing, the big, black, hairy thing, was still there standing underneath the cheese plant, glaring at us, like my worst nightmare multiplied by a trillion trillion, then another trillion thrown in.

I wanted to scream as loud as Jamie was screaming, but my throat was dry and my mouth wouldn't move. Nothing would move. I was totally frozen in the doorway.

OK, it wasn't real, the creature wasn't real. It couldn't be real. This was impossible, even for Hal. It was some sort of hologram, computer image or projection. Hal's idea of a joke maybe, only Hal doesn't do jokes.

Joke, hologram or not, it was starting to crawl towards us. Nearer and nearer, its hairs bristling. Then it stopped and crouched, as if getting ready to jump.

I had to save Jamie, I absolutely had to move. With a massive burst of energy, as if one of Hal's scary potions was exploding inside me, I leaped back, slammed the door and leaned against it, my heart thumping so hard I could hear it above Jamie's cries.

BOOM...
BOOM...
BOOM!

And with the thudding came the thoughts. Mum might be trapped in there, in Hal's bedroom, with that thing in the lab ready to pounce.

Or maybe it had eaten her and Hal already!

"**MUUUUUUUM!**"

THREE

"Anna, what on earth's going on? It sounds as though someone's being murdered down there. Is Jamie all right?"

Mum's voice was followed by the sound of feet clomping down the basement steps. Keeping my back firmly against the lab door, I looked up. It was her, it was really her!

"Mum!" I yelped, as she started unfastening Jamie's sling and tying it round her own shoulders. "You're safe."

"Of course I'm safe. Why shouldn't I be safe?"

"But where've you been? I've been looking all over!"

"I just nipped out to the post box, but never mind about me," she said, cuddling Jamie, who immediately stopped howling. "What about you? You look like you're about to throw up. Don't you feel well?"

"In there," I said, nodding back towards the door. "Something's in there. It's a . . . I think it's a sp . . . sp . . . a gi . . ."

The thought of those legs, those bulging eyes, the twitching fangs, that great, fat body with its black hairs all bristling, set me off shaking.

"Giant spider!" I managed to blurt out.

"Oh, sweetheart," said Mum, laughing and nudging me out of the way. "You're making all this fuss over a silly spider."

"Don't go in there!" I yelled, as she put her hand on the handle.

I tried to pull Mum away, without hurting Jamie, but as I tugged, the door opened and we both stumbled inside. The first thing I saw was Hal standing right in front of us, yawning and rubbing his hands through his dark brown hair. He was wearing torn black shorts and a grubby grey T-shirt that he'd obviously slept in.

"What's wrong?" he grunted. "What are you doing? Can't you read?" he added, nodding at the KEEP OUT sign.

"Er, Anna thought she saw something," Mum said. "I was just checking."

I looked past Hal to the cheese plant. There was no sign of the creature. Surely I hadn't imagined it? Or maybe Hal was the creature and the creature was Hal? Transformed like Spider-Man or something? No, that was just too freaky!

As I was shaking my head and nibbling my nails, a box suddenly moved. The enormous spider ran out from behind it and scurried under the table.

Mum screamed.

I pointed.

Jamie howled.

"Shush!" Hal said, dropping to his knees, peering under the table. "You'll frighten her."

"Frighten *her*!" I yelled. "You know about that thing?"

"Course," said Hal, still on his knees.

"So she's like a toy, right?" I said. "You've made her. She's got a computer chip or something?"

"No."

"She's not real?" I said, shaking my head again. "She can't be real."

"Come on, Tula," Hal said, far more interested in the spider than in answering me. "I won't let them hurt you."

The massive spider started to crawl out from under the table. Hal stood up while me and Mum

HUh!

edged backwards, bumping into each other, treading on each other's toes.

"Oh, stop making a fuss," Hal said as the spider slumped at his feet. "She's harmless, look. She's a House Spider."

"That is not a house spider!" I said. "House spiders are small and—"

"I don't mean an *ordinary* house spider, obviously," said Hal, as if I was totally brainless.

"So what *do* you mean?" Mum asked, swaying from side to side and patting Jamie's back in an attempt to soothe him to sleep.

Hal gave a deep sigh. "Keep quiet," he said, picking up the bag of peanuts from the table. "And I'll show you."

I had no idea what Hal was going to do with the peanuts and his furry friend but I just knew I wasn't going to like it.

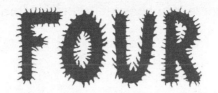

FOUR

Hal scooped a large handful of peanuts out of the bag and put them in a jam jar. He picked up a tin of pins, tipped some into the jar with the peanuts, screwed on the lid and shook it up.

"Hang on," said Mum, as the spider stood up and started to stretch, making my stomach do triple somersaults. "I mean, what exactly is that thing? Where's it come from?"

"Stop calling her a thing!" said Hal. "She's sensitive and very intelligent."

"Yes, but . . ." Mum began.

Hal gave another of his deep sighs, as if he wished we were as smart as his huge, hairy pet.

"Remember that tarantula Dad brought home from work last month?" he said.

I nodded. I'd only glanced at it once, before Hal mercifully took it off to his bedroom. But I remembered it had been in a glass tank and it wasn't the size of a cat. Bigger and hairier than your average spider, granted, but not that big!

"Well, she was really sickly," Hal said. "She hadn't been looked after properly. Owner didn't want her any more – you know what it's like. Anyway, I couldn't get her to eat, so I tried her with some new stuff I've been giving my plants."

"What sort of stuff?" I asked, keeping my

eyes on the spider, which was still standing near Hal.

"Nothing you'd understand," Hal mumbled.

"Try me."

"All right, it's just a couple of basic PGRs."

"What?"

"Plant Growth Regulators. See, I said you wouldn't get it!"

OK, he'd lost me already but I wasn't going to admit it. So I just nodded and tried to look intelligent, as he went on to explain exactly what they were. After what felt like three hours but was probably only a minute or so, Hal paused and took a deep breath.

"And the really clever bit is," he said, "I mixed in some synthetic polypeptides!"

Uh, sin polly what?

"Just a touch," Hal added, as if that made a difference; as if that gave me the faintest clue what he was on about. He looked at our blank faces and sighed. "You've heard of steroids, right, and growth hormones?"

"You used a growth hormone," said Mum. "You mean like a *human* growth hormone?"

"Sort of," said Hal. "Anyway, it worked! I must have got just the right amounts of everything because Tula really brightened up."

"And grew?" Mum said.

"Yeah, but the size isn't really important," Hal said, as though a cat-sized tarantula was perfectly fine. "It's what she can do that's amazing. Watch!"

He shook the jam jar again. Then he took off the lid and tipped the jar up, scattering pins and peanuts onto the floor. The spider reared on her two back legs. Mum clutched my arm, digging her nails in so tight that I squealed.

"Stop panicking," Hal said. "She won't hurt you. She's a Brazilian Black. They're very easy-going – nicest of all the tarantulas."

Oh, that was all right then!

"There are hundreds of different types of

tarantula," Hal added.

Like I needed a lesson on spiders! All I was bothered about was the massive spider monster in front of me right now.

While Hal was speaking, the spider stopped rearing and pounced. My stomach was still whirling like a tumble dryer but I had to admit my freaky stepbrother was right. It was pretty amazing! With two of her legs, Tula was picking up pins, popping them back in their tin, while with another two she was stuffing peanuts into her mouth.

"You see," said Hal, his green eyes glinting in that manic way of his. "House Spider! Housework problems solved. This could make us mega rich. I mean, everyone's going to want one, aren't they?"

"No!" I squealed. "No one in their right

mind's going to want a giant spider scampering around. No matter how many peanuts she picks up!"

Ignoring me again, Hal moved towards Mum, grabbing the duster and polish that were sticking out of her jacket pocket. He gave them to Tula, who ran up the rough basement wall and started dusting a shelf.

"I've been training her," Hal announced. "She loves housework. And that's not all. There's no end to what I could teach her. She's smarter than any dog. Tula!" he called, "Show me three."

The spider waved three legs.

"OK," said Hal. "Two and another two."

Four legs started to wave.

"Great," I said, wanting to vomit every time Tula moved. "Fine! But why would anyone want a giant counting spider? I mean, what's wrong with a calculator?"

"It's not just the counting," said Hal. "Think what else she could do — ironing, washing up, rocking the baby."

"Are you mad?" I yelled, sidling round to stand in front of Mum. "No way is she coming near Jamie."

"Whatever," said Hal, "but House Spiders would be dead cheap and imagine the energy they'd save. The green solution to housework! No more noisy vacuum cleaners or dishwashers eating up electricity. Totally environmentally friendly! And they'd keep the flies down, so no need for nasty sprays. Think about it."

Oh, I was thinking about it, all right. And Hal was completely, totally, absolutely beyond crazy if he thought he was going to breed a houseful of giant tarantulas.

One was too many.

I glared at Hal, then turned to Mum.

"Either that thing goes," I said, "or I do! And I'll be taking Jamie with me."

FIVE

Rain trickled off my fringe and ran down my nose, but at least Jamie was safe and warm in his buggy.

"Anna, get in the car," Steve pleaded.

"This is silly," Mum said. "Where would you go?"

"Gran and Grandad's," I muttered.

"They're in the middle of the Pacific on a cruise," Mum said.

OK, so I hadn't thought things out very well or got very far. I'd left early on Sunday morning but I was barely at the top of our lane when they caught up with me.

"It'll be fine, honestly," Steve said. "Tula might look a bit gross but she really is harmless."

A bit gross didn't even start to cover it, but we couldn't upset Hal, could we?

Oh no, Hal's brilliant, Hal's a genius, Hal can do what he likes. If Hal wants ginormous spiders scurrying around eating babies and all our pets, then that's fine, isn't it?

"I've had a talk with Hal," Steve said. "I've explained that the world probably isn't ready for giant House Spiders. So he won't rear any more. And he's promised to keep Tula safely locked in the basement."

"Are you sure?"

"Yes," Steve said. "I promise. Come on, Anna. You can't leave home and you certainly can't take Jamie. He needs his mum."

"Fine," I muttered.

Well, what else could I do? I had nowhere to go and Steve was right. I couldn't look after Jamie on my own.

Jamie was sleeping when we got back so I left him in his buggy, in the kitchen with Mum, while I went upstairs. As I was coming out of the bathroom, fairly dry again, the house phone rang.

Mum picked up down in the hall, so I headed for my room – and saw Hal coming out! What was going on? Hal hardly ever leaves the basement and he'd never, ever, been in my room before.

"Don't suppose you've seen Tula?" he said, looking down at his trainers.

"WHAT?"

"I can't seem to find her."

Oh no! She'd got out already. I might have known!

"What about Jamie?" I yelped.

"It's all right," Hal said. "Your mum's with him."

"No, she isn't. Mum!" I shouted, running down the stairs. "Check Jamie – quick!"

"Uh," said Mum, dropping the phone as I rushed past her towards the kitchen.

The kitchen door was open and there, on the work surface near the sink, was the spider. With one leg she was pushing a dishcloth around, cleaning the sink. But another two legs were wrapped round the handle of Jamie's buggy and she was pulling it towards her!

"Get her away from him," I shouted, as Hal and Mum turned up.

"What's the problem?" said Hal.

See what I mean about Hal? There's a huge tarantula holding Jamie's buggy and he asks what the problem is!

"She's only rocking it," said Hal. "Look, they like each other," he added, as Tula jumped down to the floor.

I looked closer. Jamie was gurgling, laughing

and stretching out his little hand to stroke the spider's leg. Oh, yuck! And the spider kept tilting her head, as if she was smiling at Jamie. Or maybe she was just hungry . . .

"No," I said, as Tula's fangs twitched. "Get her away. She's dangerous. She's evil. She's horrible."

"Oh, stop being so hysterical, Anna," said Hal.

The spider leaped up. She dropped the dishcloth in the sink and moved away from the buggy. Then she slumped on the kitchen surface, looking at me with misty eyes – two big ones and six smaller ones all looking really, really sad. I swear she was trying to make me feel guilty!

"See, you've upset her," said Hal, scooping Tula up in his arms.

He actually picked her up and hugged her! I'd never seen Hal hug anyone or anything before, not even his dad.

"I do think you're overreacting, Anna," Mum said, as Hal stormed out with the spider draped round his neck and I threw up on the kitchen floor.

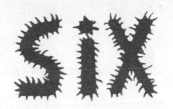

SIX

"Goodness, Anna," Miss Bradshaw said, as I stumbled into class on Monday morning. "You look awful, er, awfully pale. Don't you feel well?"

No, because I've been up all night worrying about being eaten alive by a giant spider didn't seem the right sort of answer somehow.

Nima and Joe started fussing round me when I slumped down at our table. Even Max, who doesn't usually notice anything, asked me what was wrong. But Steve had told me not to mention Tula so I just gave a weak

smile and said, "It's nothing, I'm fine," and tried to get on with my work.

Not that I could concentrate. All I could think about was Mum and Jamie back home. Steve was working, it was one of Hal's school days and Tula was supposed to be locked in a large cat pen in Hal's lab, but what if she got out? If she was as smart as Hal said, she could probably pick locks!

At break I sent Mum a text. At lunch I sent four more and the answer was always the same: stop worrying, she and Jamie were fine. Even so, when I got off the school bus that afternoon, I ran all the way down our lane.

Panting, I burst in through the back door and, yes! There was Mum and Jamie building towers of colourful, plastic bricks on the floor.

There was no sign of Tula until after dinner when Hal brought her up to the kitchen.

"Wow," said Mum, as Tula collected up the plates and started running water in the sink, while shoving bits of leftover food into her mouth. "Waste disposal and washing up all at the same time."

Jamie giggled as Tula started blowing bubbles towards him with the washing-up liquid.

POP!

"Amazing," said Steve, sidling up to the sink to watch. "Come and see how gentle she is, Anna. And the plates are so clean!"

"No thanks," I mumbled, already halfway out the door.

Even homework was better than watching everyone fussing round the hairy horror. No way could I cope with that thing in the house. What on earth was I going to do? I stomped upstairs, flung open my bedroom door and stared.

Oh wow, had Tula done all this? It wouldn't be Mum or Steve, because we were supposed to look after our own rooms, but the clothes I'd left on the floor had all been picked up and were neatly folded on my bed. My furniture was gleaming, my carpet was spotless and my waste bin had been emptied.

I flopped down at my desk, which was tidy for the first time ever with all my homework books already laid out. OK, maybe, just maybe, I could get used to having a House Spider – if only she wasn't quite so hairy scary!

My homework didn't take long but I was really tired. What I needed was a nice bath and an early night. I picked up a magazine and wandered into the bathroom, reading the problem page. Still reading, I reached towards the bath taps and touched something furry.

"Aaaaaaaaargh," I yelped, as Tula leaped right out of the bath and clung to the curtain rail with two legs, while the others dangled, clutching cloths, sponges and lemon-scented bath spray.

It gave a whole new meaning to finding a spider in the bath – that was for sure.

My magazine had flown out of my hand and dropped down the loo. It was useless, anyway. The problems were all about boyfriends, spots and irritating parents – absolutely no advice on giant spiders or strange stepbrothers!

"Anna," said Hal, arriving at the bathroom door. "You've scared Tula again!"

I'd scared *her*? Yeah, right.

"What is it with her, anyway?" I said. "How come she's so housework-obsessed? Was it something to do with those growth thingies?"

"No, I don't reckon," said Hal, as he tried to coax Tula down. "Most spiders make fantastic webs or line their dens with silk, don't they?"

I didn't know much about den-making spiders, like tarantulas, but I'd seen enough webs and they do have amazing patterns.

"Right," I said, trying to get my head round

it. "So you think spiders are, like, naturally house-proud?"

"Yeah, it makes sense."

Hal has a funny idea of sense!

"But most spiders don't go around polishing and spraying their webs, do they?" I pointed out.

"So?" said Hal. "Wild dolphins don't balance balls on their noses, but they do in zoos and stuff! To train an animal, you just use its basic skills and go from there. I showed Tula what to do and she loves it!"

"Great, fine," I said, backing away as Tula finally dropped down, "but just get her out of here."

My heart drummed a loud beat as I marched back to my room to pick up my pyjamas and stuff. I did everything slowly, giving them plenty of time to leave, but when I got back, they were still there.

"We're just going," Hal said, "but Tula wanted to . . ."

He nodded towards the bath, which Tula had filled with loads of foamy water, just how I like it. As she was leaving, she picked up Jamie's yellow plastic duck and popped it in the water. Then she gave a little wave with one of her legs and winked with one of her eyes.

My heart was still thudding away but I laughed. I just couldn't help it.

Who'd believe it? A giant House Spider with a sense of humour!

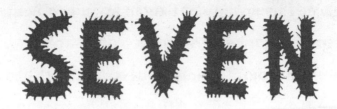

SEVEN

A black, hairy leg stretched towards me. I took a deep breath, then grabbed the beautifully ironed school shirt, which was dangling from the foot.

"Thanks," I said, draping the shirt over the back of the kitchen chair.

Tula waved her leg, as if to say "It's a pleasure", while I went back to my laptop, as if a spider doing the ironing was the most normal thing ever.

It's totally amazing what you can get used to. Trust me! It was only Thursday and I could already be in the same room as Tula without screaming or being sick. I wouldn't stroke her, like Mum did. I certainly never cuddled her, like Hal. And I insisted that she didn't get too close to Jamie but, mainly, we'd started to get along.

"She really is a big help," Mum said, as Tula handed her a pile of neatly ironed knickers. "I'd never have believed it."

Well, I couldn't argue with any of that.

I looked down at my laptop, where I was checking out tarantulas. Then I glanced up at Hal, who was filming Tula as she happily counted out eight carrots and four large potatoes for dinner.

"OK, so even if spiders are naturally house-proud," I said. "What about that? Do most spiders sit around counting their flies?"

"They might do," said Hal. "Who's to say? Spiders are definitely smart. It's just more obvious now Tula's bigger and the HGH probably gave her brain a boost."

While I was working out that HGH was probably the Human Growth Hormone, Tula stretched out a leg, grabbed a bluebottle off the window and popped it in her mouth.

"Don't let her near the window during daytime," Steve said.

"No problem," said Hal. "She mainly sleeps during the day."

"And we should keep the curtains shut when she's up here. People can be funny about anything a bit unusual," Steve added.

Well, yes, our Tula was certainly unusual!

"And we wouldn't want anyone to hurt you, would we, Tula?" Steve said, wandering over to stroke her head.

"Hey, you haven't told anyone about Tula, have you?" said Hal, swinging round to glare at me. "At school or anything?"

"No! Why would I? I'm not stupid."

Who'd believe me, for a start? Well, actually they might if I said it had something to do with Hal. It seems his experiments have been causing chaos since he was in Infants.

Amazingly, though, some of Hal's inventions have actually worked. Hal's even sold stuff to big companies for a fair bit of money, Steve says, but it's the disasters that people around here remember. Was Tula going to be one of the disasters? Yet she *was* helpful and Hal seemed loads happier since he'd started the Tula project.

Well, as happy as Hal ever gets. He'd even started coming up to eat with us, so I was surprised on Saturday evening when Steve took Hal's sausage and mash down to the basement. He even took two extra sausages for Tula. That was definitely one good thing about Tula – she wasn't a fussy eater. She'd happily munch anything from flies to cat food to spaghetti hoops, but sausages seemed to be her favourite.

"Is Hal not coming up?" Mum asked when Steve came back.

"No, he's in the middle of another experiment. New kind of bio-fuel, I think."

I didn't bother asking for details. Hal's experiments are way beyond me. And at least bio-fuel sounded better than giant spiders.

Or at least that's what I thought, until later when I was getting ready for bed and . . . Bang! There was some sort of explosion from the basement.

Grabbing my jeans and jumper, I struggled back into my clothes then stumbled down to the hall. Mum was clutching Jamie. Steve was fussing around Hal, who was covered in green slime and had a cut on his cheek.

"It's nothing," Hal said, shrugging. "No real damage. Mainly just noise – but it scared Tula. She got out."

"OK," said Steve, starting to look around the hall. "We'll find her."

"No, I mean *out*," said Hal. "The window was open."

Oh, great, just great!

Five minutes later, me, Steve and a still slightly slimy Hal were out on the lane, in coats and wellies, with our torches, searching for a very big, black spider on a very dark, drizzly night. We don't have street lamps in our village but, luckily, we don't have many neighbours either.

Up one end of the lane there's a group of six houses, and at the other end there's a farm. Our house is in the middle, and apart from that it's all fields. Hal headed off towards the houses, Steve leaped over a fence into a field, which left me to walk towards the farm.

"Tula," I hissed, waving my torch, hoping she wasn't going to drop out of a tree or anything.

I might have got used to her, even fond of her in a funny sort of way, but that didn't mean I wanted her dropping on my head. Even worse, what if she got into someone's house and gave them a heart attack or something? Would we be charged with murder?

"Baaaaaaaaaaaaaaaaaaaa."

The lane was suddenly full of the sound of manic bleating and I could hear someone yelling from the direction of the farm.

Oh no, surely Tula wasn't chasing sheep!

Tucking the torch under my arm, I pulled my mobile from my pocket. Just as I was gabbling at Steve, something wet brushed past my legs and I swung round to see Tula racing towards home.

"Ah, it's OK," I told Steve.

We agreed to meet back at the house. But, as I was putting my phone away, I realised I wasn't alone.

Looking up, I saw a shotgun pointing at my chest.

EIGHT

Behind the shotgun was Farmer Bull. Yes, he really is called Mr Bull and he looks like one as well. So big and fierce, you'd expect to see a ring through his nose. Next to him was his daughter, Sulky Sarah, the only person in my class I don't like.

"Where is it?" Bull asked. He lowered the gun as Sarah shone her torch all around.

"Where's what?"

"Don't play dumb," Bull snarled. "We saw it! It was chasing our sheep. This is something to do with your crazy brother, isn't it?"

"Stepbrother," I said. "So you think Hal's been chasing your sheep?"

"Not Hal," said Bull. "The giant spider that's just run towards your house."

"Spider?" I said, with my best smirk.

"Don't try and deny it," said Bull. "Daft as it seems, it's no dafter than purple goats."

Huh? Purple goats, what was he on about?

"I know what I saw," he went on, "and I'm calling the police."

★

Back at the house, Hal was cuddling a rather soggy spider. Steve started pacing as I told them what had happened.

"Bull's just a nutter," said Hal. "And he hates me."

"I don't think he hates you, exactly," said Steve.

"He does!"

"Er, it wouldn't have anything to do with purple goats, would it?" I asked.

"Oh, that," said Hal with a shrug. "New animal shampoo I gave Bull to try. It was great. Smelled of lavender, killed off any creepy-crawlies and made the fur really, really glossy."

"So, shiny but purple?" I said.

"Bit of a mix-up with the ingredients,"

said Hal. "But it's not like it was permanent or anything. It wore off after a few weeks."

"Yes, but by then he'd missed the County Show," Steve said.

"Anyway," said Hal, "that was ages ago. I was only eight – long time to bear a grudge!"

"Mmm, but to be fair it wasn't just his prize goats, was it?" said Steve, drying Tula's legs with a towel. "He missed the sheep-dog trials as well."

"He could still have entered," said Hal.

"I guess he'd have felt kind of silly with a black and purple collie," Steve pointed out. "And then there was that business with the poisonous pond weed a couple of years back."

"That was so not my fault!"

Hal's fault or not, I was starting to see why Bull was being so nasty and why Sarah spent most of her time at school scowling at me.

"He's lying, anyway," Hal said, holding Tula close. "You wouldn't hurt his stupid sheep, would you, poppet? She was probably just playing."

"Yes, but try proving it," Mum said. "And what if the police come round?"

"Like the cops are going to believe him," said Hal. "They'll just think he's been at the whisky."

"Maybe," said Steve. "But Bull's got a way of making people do what he wants."

"So, we'll hide her," said Hal.

"They might search the house," said Mum.

"And if they find her," said Steve, "they'll have her put down."

"No way!" said Hal, as Tula started to shiver, all eight legs quivering.

Did Tula understand? I wasn't sure. And OK, so I still found her scary, but I really, really didn't want anyone to hurt her.

"Even if they don't find her tonight, we won't be able to keep her secret for ever. Not now Bull's seen her," Steve said, as the doorbell rang.

"Keep them talking," said Hal, darting off towards the basement with Tula.

I followed Steve to the door and the moment he opened it Bull barged in, still clutching his shotgun.

"Police are on their way," he said, looking around the hall.

"So, were any of your sheep actually hurt?" Steve asked.

"No," said Bull. "But they might have been. That thing could have killed the whole flock!"

"Er, maybe it was a fox you saw," I said.

"With eight legs?" Bull snapped.

"Makes as much sense as a massive spider," Steve said.

"Well, whatever it was," said Bull, waving his gun around, "it came in here. And when I find it, I'll blast it to pieces!"

Through the hall window I saw the glare of headlights and heard a car drawing up. The police were here. It was time to see if Hal had managed to hide Tula.

While Steve tried to offer Bull a nice, calming cup of herbal tea, I slipped off to the basement.

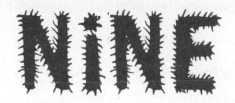

NiNE

"Not exactly well hidden, is she?" I said, looking at Tula, who was sitting on the table right in the middle of Hal's lab, which was full of slime and messier than ever after the explosion.

Tula was making a bit of an effort to tidy up but I could see she was worried.

"Shh," said Hal, picking up a plastic bottle from the floor. "I'm thinking."

"Well, you'd better hurry up."

Hal's face turned pale as he looked at the pinkish liquid in the bottle. Then he opened a desk drawer and took out one of the droppers I've seen Steve use when he's giving our pets eye drops.

"What are you doing?" I asked.

"Nothing, I hope," Hal said. "Text your mum, find out what's going on."

"What's that stuff," I asked, nodding at the bottle as I tapped in my text.

"A reducing agent," Hal whispered, glancing at Tula and opening the bottle.

"A what?"

"Reducing agent – makes things smaller."

"You mean you could get her back to normal size! But that's great."

"It's new. It hasn't been properly tested," said Hal, speaking quickly, like he does when he gets really wound up. "Might not work, might not work fast enough. Not sure how much to use. I'll have to guess. It might harm her. Might even kill her! No, I can't risk it."

"You'll have to," I said, looking at the text Mum had sent. "The police haven't got a search warrant but Bull's stomping around up there, demanding to look around. Oh no," I added as another text popped up.

"Bull's stormed out of the kitchen – says he's going to find the spider himself!"

"Right," said Hal. "I need you to hold Tula."

"Hold her?" I squeaked. "Me? Couldn't we get Steve?"

"No time," said Hal, "and if Dad came down here, Bull would too."

"Look, can't we just hide Tula for now?" I tried. "Shove her in a box under the table or disguise her as a plant or something?"

"Too late, too risky," said Hal, as we heard footsteps overhead, clomping towards the basement door, and the sound of voices arguing. "Quick, lock the lab door."

I turned round and pulled a bolt across.

"Now hold Tula," Hal said. "And do it properly. I don't want to make a mistake."

I edged closer. Tula saw Hal fill the dropper

from the bottle and now started waving her legs around. Two of her eyes seemed to have grown extra huge, the hairs on her back were bristling and her fangs were twitching. I couldn't do it. I couldn't touch her. I couldn't.

"Just put your arms round her. Keep her still while I open her mouth and give her the drops," Hal snapped. "She won't harm you! Even if she bites, her poison won't be fatal – I don't think."

"Poison?" I yelped. "Fatal! You mean it could kill me?"

"Unlikely," Hal said, as if he didn't much care either way. "Normal tarantula bites are just like bee stings but with her being a bit bigger . . ."

A bit bigger! A bite from Tula could

probably take off my hand.

"It's all right," Hal was saying in a much softer voice to Tula. "It'll be better like this. Keep you safe, eh? We won't let that nasty man hurt you. I'll be careful. I'll get the dose right. I promise."

I edged towards them. Then, hearing footsteps on the stairs, I threw my arms round Tula and closed my eyes.

"Hal, have you done it yet?" I whispered when someone started banging on the lab door.

"Yes."

"Has it worked?"

It still felt as if I was holding a very large and nervous spider.

"I don't know," Hal hissed. "I think something might be happening – look."

"Open this door!" Farmer Bull yelled.

I let go of Tula, opened my eyes and stood back. Was it my imagination or was she just a teeny weeny bit smaller?

"I said, open up!" Bull shouted over a babble of other voices, including little Jamie wailing.

I looked at Tula again. It was no good. Even if she was getting smaller, it wasn't working fast enough.

Hal shoved the dropper and the bottle into a drawer, picked up Tula, headed towards his bedroom and nodded at me.

"Hold them off as long as you can," he mouthed before disappearing into his room with Tula.

"All right, I'm coming," I called, pulling on the bolt very, very slowly, as the banging started again.

Crowded into the small space between the basement steps and the lab door were Mum, who was holding Jamie, then Steve, a policeman, a police lady and a red-faced, wild-eyed Farmer Bull, mercifully without his shotgun. At least he wouldn't be able to shoot Tula.

"Where is it?" said Bull, pushing past me

and looking around the lab.

"Er, Hal's gone for a lie down," I said, moving between Bull and the bedroom door. "He's got a headache."

"I don't care about Hal or his headache! What's he done with that thing?"

HUMPh!

"Mr Bull thinks you might be keeping a dangerous animal down here," the policeman said, picking a skull up off the table, and looking around at the slimy mess.

"We've checked the rest of the house," said the police lady, yawning and looking at her watch.

"Careful where you're treading," Steve told the officers. "Hal keeps all sorts down here but not, as far as I know, any dangerous beasts."

They were all slowly moving closer to Hal's room. Had Tula got any smaller? Would Hal have had time to hide her? Or might we all end up in prison for keeping a wild animal?

And just what would happen to poor Tula?

TEN

"Is that the bedroom?" the police lady asked, as I stood in front of the door, with Bull looming over me. "Can we go in?"

"Hal?" I called. "The police want to look in your room."

"Oh, right. OK, won't be a minute."

The minute seemed to stretch for ever, with Bull moving from foot to foot, huffing and snorting. Then, finally, Hal flung the door open, standing back to let us all look inside. Unlike the lab, Hal's bedroom was very tidy. Perhaps Tula had been at work, but there wasn't much in there anyway. So it didn't take Bull long to barge in, open the wardrobe, peer under the bed and check the shower room.

"No giant spiders, sir?" the police lady asked.

I looked towards the glass tank on top of Hal's chest of drawers. The tank was full of plants, stones and a small, hollow log.

"Oh, you're looking for a big spider?" Hal said. "Is this the one?"

He put his hand into the tank, lifted out the log and tipped a tarantula onto the palm of his hand. The police lady squeaked and the policeman stepped back.

"It's certainly big," the policeman said, looking at Bull, "but I can't see it being a danger to your sheep."

"That's not the one!" Bull said. "That's just an ordinary tarantula. The one I saw was this big," he added, stretching his arms out wide.

The police lady was trying hard not to laugh.

"You haven't heard the last of this," Bull snarled at us, before storming out. "You wait and see!"

"That was brill," I said to Hal, after everyone had gone. "You did it! Tula's safe."

"I don't know," he said, gazing at the spider lying very still on his hand. "She doesn't look at all well now. Maybe I gave her too much, too quickly."

"She'll be fine," I said. "I'm sure she'll be fine."

I noticed a tear drip onto the log when Hal put Tula back in her tank.

"I think she's dying," Hal said.

"This is madness," Mum announced, when I got home from school on Wednesday evening.

"Tula's not eating, Hal's not eating and I can't get him out of that flaming basement at all."

"He's working on something to try and make Tula better," said Steve, who was lying on the floor, playing baby games with Jamie.

"Hopefully nothing to make her grow again," Mum said. "I could do without more visits from the police – although I do miss the help around the house!"

"Mmm," said Steve. "Tula certainly seemed healthier and happier when she was bigger, but it's too risky."

Something clicked in my brain. Something Hal had said that Saturday morning when he was demonstrating the brilliance of House Spiders.

The size isn't really important.

"So what if Tula's not actually sick?" I asked Steve.

"Uh," said Steve, as Jamie grabbed at his nose.

"I've got an idea," I said. "Could you get something from the loft for me?" And I told him what I wanted.

While Steve was in the loft, I went to see Tula, who was curled up in her log with her dish of food untouched.

"It's my fault," said Hal. "That stuff I gave her must have made her ill again."

He didn't look too good himself. He was even paler than usual with dark rings under his eyes. There was no point trying to reason with him. We'd all tried during the week. I just had to wait for Steve to turn up, and hope my idea worked.

Steve finally staggered through and dumped a big box on the floor.

"A doll's house," Hal said, as I started unpacking it. "You've brought me a doll's house?"

"It's not for you," I said, setting it up in the corner of his room.

For a genius, he can be a bit dim at times.

"It's for Tula," I announced. "I don't think she's sick. She's just unhappy and bored. You taught her all that stuff, but now she can't do anything."

"Bored," Steve said, shaking his head as if I was mad.

But when I turned towards Tula's tank, I knew I wasn't mad. She was out of her log, trying to scramble up the side of the glass. Hal lifted Tula out and popped her into the

87

doll's house, where she immediately started scurrying around straightening the little rugs and rocking the tiny doll in its pram.

I have to say, it's a pretty smart doll's house. Gran bought it for my fifth birthday.

It's got three floors, a bathroom to clean, some lovely wooden furniture to polish and beds with real bedclothes for Tula to tidy. All it needed now were some bits of material I'd cut up for dusters.

The corners of Hal's mouth twitched, which is about as near as he ever gets to a smile, when I put Tula's food in the kitchen and she started to eat.

So now we've got a very happy tarantula, living in a doll's house, and life's got back to normal.

But with Hal starting work on a new, secret experiment, I'm not sure how long peace will last . . .